The Memory Extracts

A Companion Anthology to The Vending Portal

Judy Liu

Dedicated to my bug, my mom and dad, Mildred (even though she just needs to exist and stare at me with her boba eyes), my community of friends who stand behind me, the women in my life who replenish my soul, and to my fearless 7-year old self who if it weren't for remembering her, I would not be where I am now.

Contents

Note to the Reader

Welcome to the culmination of what was an experimental passion project. *The Memory Extracts* is a collection of memories from citizens who live in or are associated with the Second Layer of the world from my debut novel, *The Vending Portal*. The world is an advanced society of marine technology with one fatal flaw: that its people start losing their memories upon turning 18 years of age, with children being highly mentally developed.

Feel free to read this with or without having read *The Vending Portal*!

These are all extractions pulled from MAGMA, the Multiplex Archive owned by the Government Memory Association, which was created to help its citizens retain their memories as they age with government science and drugs.

As such, I hope you find this short anthology a fun companion work to *The Vending Portal* as we take momentary glimpses into the everyday lives of people.

THE BOOTLEGGER ON THE PRECIPICE

"Ironic, isn't it?" Calvin thought to himself as he added two stalks of red algae to his tisane, an herbal infusion made by steeping a variety of plants, bark, fruit, and spices in hot water for medicinal purposes. In Calvin's case, he was concocting a tisane for memory recall and retention.

Calvin ran his own apothecary from the decrepit Multiplex Archive building. The building was still owned by the Government Memory Association ('GMA' for short), but they have forgotten about it for as long as Calvin could remember. He found it funny that the GMA, who flaunted themselves as the savior of the public's declining memories, would forget about their own building. Luckily for Calvin, this worked out for him.

This MAGMA building, just one of the hundreds that belong to the government hence its acronym being a combination of the building Multiplex Archive and government GMA abbreviation, has served as Calvin's safe space over the years. It was a place he could sit for hours, helping those less privileged while making a small buck for himself. But now, his usually discreet business was booming. He could barely meet demand.

He picked a few sage leaves and added them to the mixture while muttering to himself.

"If you told me the enforcer unit would commit treason to arrest the Prime Minister two weeks ago, I would have never believed it." He turned on his gas stove and placed a pot of dark liquid on top.

A chime jingled above his head, indicating someone had placed another order for his memory tisanes. Calvin had been receiving endless orders ever since news broke about the Prime Minister. With the GMA thrown into chaos, it was having challenges with its Reminserum supply. As a result, some people were looking for alternatives, and this was where Calvin's tisanes came in. They were not as potent as the lab-created Reminserum and there was no way someone could rely solely on his tisanes, but his customers were happy.

All right. As that order is steeping, let's move onto the next before I close up shop. Calvin pulled the order slip down from the line he had running through the building and snaking outside. This was how people requested orders since Calvin made it a principle to never meet his clients face-to-face. This order was in a familiar neat scrawl. Calvin scowled at it.

"Not this client again..." He didn't know his clients by name, but he knew them by their handwriting, and this person was *not* one of his regulars. They had shown up a week ago, pounding on his MAGMA doors, demanding to meet. When he didn't, they had left the largest order Calvin had ever received, which resulted in a significant delay to his other clients. This person didn't respect his process either then, sending daily messages to pester him about their order.

This person is probably not lacking in money and accustomed to using Reminserum and getting what they want. And that's *why this person has zero tact when it comes to an underground business, like my own...* Calvin was used to working for people like himself, and even though helping the socially elite left a bad taste in his mouth, it was undeniably good business.

He exhaled in annoyance and tossed the slip with the neat handwriting aside while getting up. *The rich can wait.* He'd much rather check on his plants before locking up.

Calvin worked in the large central opening of the MAGMA building. He had a desk in the middle of the spacious atrium with a table next to it that had a row of three portable stoves. His whole setup was surrounded by tall shelves of vertical farms. Despite the enormity of the MAGMA building with its labyrinth of rooms, Calvin only used this open atrium and a special room in the basement: a 6.3 million gallon aquatic tank, large enough to fit up to six full-size whale sharks. He didn't keep whale sharks in there, however.

He went downstairs to check on the massive aquarium he inherited and was met by the familiar feeling of stepping into a muffled, underwater forest, the dim blue light filtering through the leafy 70-foot tall stalks of kelp, resulting in the light dancing gently across the floor and reflecting off his face.

There was nothing he loved more than donning on the diving drysuit and dropping into the depths of the tank, swimming among the stalks of kelp that gently waved back and forth, the leaves embracing him as he swam by with small schools of fish. When floating among the kelp, Calvin shed all the responsibilities he shouldered and felt free. He felt anything was possible.

He spent a few seconds absorbing this feeling before making his way to the side room that was filled with gauges. He was fortunately a quick read, and with a few books from the library and common sense, Calvin self-taught himself how to read these gauges and what the kelp needed.

Thank goodness MAGMA built this thoroughly. If something were really *to go wrong with the tank, I wouldn't be able to fix it.* All Calvin could do was watch the gauges to know if something was wrong or not, and over these last six years, everything has functioned as it should. Every day, he prayed to Mazu, the sea goddess, that nothing would go wrong with this tank because he needed the kelp for his tisanes. He only knew how to harvest the kelp, but there was no way he could identify any root cause of atypical water levels or disease and fix it. However, this was the least of his worries this year with his eighteenth birthday coming, marking his looming loss of Kanperetinentia. He couldn't imagine the loss of his ability to remember everything to the millisecond of his life, with a reliable mental log to recall anything and revisit details. To go from *that* to adulthood when memories start to fragment was chilling, like the cold water of the depths seeping into one's bones if one didn't put on the diving suit properly.

It's already getting dark. I don't have time to go in today. Calvin regretfully went back upstairs, packed the tisane that had finished steeping, and gathered his prized books on horticulture, pharmaceuticals, and organic chemistry. As he left the building, he placed the jar of tisane behind an inconspicuous rock for his client and headed back home.

But not before running back to the nearby vending machine to grab one of his favorite treats: the packaged cinnamon buns. *With all these negative thoughts, some sugar would be nice.*

"Hey, Calvin. I was just about to call you for dinner," his mom announced as he walked through the door.

He placed his bags down and helped his mom set the table as she served up the fermented side dishes. As he got to setting her a glass of water, he slipped the contents of a small vial from his pocket into her glass. This was a flavorless tisane that he kept for himself and his mother. She wouldn't approve of his illegal activities, and he knew she worried more than enough, so he micro-dosed her whenever he could to help her in her day-to-day. She had access to MAGMA buildings and their Reminserum, but she was often too busy with her three jobs to go as regularly as an adult her age needed. Ever since he perfected his mixture and started dosing her, she had been going less and less, but didn't have the time to notice or wonder why. At first, Calvin had felt a weight on him anytime he slipped the tisane into his mom's beverages without her knowing. More than once, he'd found the urge blossoming in his chest to tell her, only to stop himself whenever he got close to doing so. He knew that if he told her, the burden then fell on her to choose between him and her civic duty that she was held to by the tenets of one of the most important pieces of literature, *How to be an Upstanding Citizen*. He'd rather shoulder this load himself and spare her. And if it was for her memory, then it should be fine. At least, that's what Calvin told himself.

Calvin had started experimenting with his memory tisanes purely out of his own interest which led to providing help for those who wanted a boost for their memories or those who didn't have the time or resources to go to MAGMA as often as needed, but with the GMA lacking a leader and trying to collect itself now, Calvin found increased significance to his work.

Who knew what would happen to Reminserum if the government didn't pull itself together?

Why did this have to happen the year I turn eighteen? While lost in thought, Calvin brushed a bowl of heaping noodles off the table, resulting in a loud crack as plastic hit the floor and food spilled everywhere.

"Calvin! Are you okay?" his mom exclaimed while bringing the remaining dishes over.

"I'm sorry. It's been a long day." As Calvin stooped to clean up his mess, a guilt tugged at Calvin's heart for wasting a bowl of food due to his being distracted. *What will Mom do once I lose Kanperetinentia, too? What will she do without my micro-doses? What would I do if I forget my recipes? Lose my notes? How can I keep improving my work without my perfect memory?*

These questions had become incessant with his upcoming birthday, and Calvin found it increasingly difficult to focus on anything else in his life.

"It's funny..." he thought to himself, "how the underground maker of a bootleg Reminserum will need to eventually rely on Reminserum himself." He cracked a bitter smile.

How ironic.

THE UNLIKELY DUO

It's not often a man puts his own life on the line for a food, but this rare eel was every bit worth the risk of lung paralyzation with the decadent flake of its tender meat that perfectly took to the chef's seasoning while shining through with its own salty, subtly bitter undertone.

T hiago Thalmang finished his sentence and closed his notebook with a satisfying *thump*. He recounted each of his adventures searching for unique foods, keeping the records for himself and for writing his later reviews.

Next up: the rumored peach tree in the middle of nowhere that produces one fruit a year. Thiago snapped his fingers and glanced at his calendar that projected onto the wall on cue. *It's almost the season the tree should be producing.* Of course, this tree wasn't in the middle of nowhere — this was just the sensational rumor. After much research, Thiago found that the tree is on an island, supposedly inhabited by a small, insular village. No one knew much about them.

"So, when are we going for that peach tree?" Benji interrupted Thiago's thoughts.

"I need to conduct some more research and preparation," Thiago replied while heading to the kitchen. Benji was his nephew who lived with him. He was around six years old, but Thiago wasn't sure since Benji never shared his birthday with him. Thiago never imagined himself living with a child, but something about Benji put him at ease.

Benji was surprisingly empathetic and situationally aware for his age. Thiago was sure this may be a result of Benji's past, but he never asked. Plus, it was nice having a human recorder around. Most adults had their children to help with memory recall issues since children still had their Kanperetinentia. Thiago wouldn't have minded not having children since he could stave off the effects of memory loss with Reminserum, but when he traversed to remote locations searching for different cuisines, he didn't always have easy access to Reminserum to aid his memories. That's when having a Benji was immensely helpful. It was an additional perk that Benji was great company, as well.

Thiago scooped some coffee beans into his mill to hand-grind. He preferred light roast and always had it black. His nephew had followed him into the kitchen, setting his prized stuffed bear into a chair at the breakfast table.

"Remember you need to bring me along this time."

"I always bring you along," Thiago retorted, transferring his ground beans to his ceramic pour-over dripper that he placed over a mug.

"Yeah, but this time, you *have* to. You're allergic to peaches. I have to be there just in case." Benji padded to the pantry to grab some canned tuna. "Tuna melt?" he held the can up to Thiago in offering.

"No, thank you. Coffee is sufficient." Thiago sighed contentedly as he poured hot water over the grinds in a gentle spiral, inhaling the aroma of the coffee that permeated the kitchen. *Yes, I know I'm allergic, but I'll have medicine on hand. And it's all worth it for this. For this mythical one-time peach.* "Just imagine," he said to Benji, closing his eyes, "what the possibilities of this peach could be if the tree puts all its efforts into producing only one. Imagine all the nutrients and energy from this large tree into this one, small fruit." He opened his eyes and looked at Benji. "*That's* what I want to experience."

To his dismay and unsurprise, Benji merely shrugged.

"I never really understood your passion for food to the point of possible death, but I'm not judging. I just don't want you to drop dead in front of me with this blissfully ignorant smile, drooling from your salivation, okay?" Benji grabbed some Sakan cheese, a cheese derived from fish collagen, from their small cheese cave to grate onto the tuna.

Now it was Thiago's turn to shrug.

"What can I say? That sounds like an amazing way to go. Coffee?" he offered to Benji. Benji threw him a dirty look before continuing.

"Are you going to regale me with the profile of this coffee if I accept it?"

"Always." Thiago grinned.

"Then, no thanks." Benji slid his tray of four slices of open-faced tuna melts into the oven and set the time.

The two of them sat in silence for a bit after that, Thiago slowly savoring his coffee, and Benji continuously checking on his tuna melts until they were toasted to the perfect melt ratio.

"You know," Benji started in-between bites, "even though I think your love for food is ridiculous, I respect your outlook on life and experiencing good things. Ever since living with you, I have come to appreciate and love simple, good food." He looked at his last slice. "Like this exquisite tuna melt, canned tuna elevated by our homemade, aged cheese on artisan bread." He beamed at Thiago.

Thiago treated Benji like an adult for the most part (most children talked like adults anyway), and moments like these reminded him that Benji — no matter how mature, thoughtful, and emotionally intelligent — was just a kid. A kid who needed a guide.

"We may need to go into town today. I need to write another review to complete my current contract." Thiago changed the subject. In his free time between travels, Thiago was a freelance food critic. However, he hasn't needed this income since he inherited his family's fortune from engineering a popular drink for the government decades ago, but he enjoyed the work and would have gone to these restaurants anyway.

Benji popped out of his chair. "I'll go get ready!" and he zoomed out of the room, stuffed bear in tow. Thiago chuckled softly as he got up to put away the dishes.

Thirty minutes later, Thiago was dressed in his usual: sandals and a weathered undershirt. He liked to keep a low profile to not draw too much attention at restaurants and bistros. However, he kept the rest of his visage impeccable: cleanly-shaven, moisturized lips, sunscreen'd, shaped brows, and a glorious pompadour hairstyle.

"I'm departing soon!" he called as Benji came speeding to the front door.

"Ready!" the child chirped excitedly. Thiago noticed Benji had tried styling his hair in a mini-pompadour and gave a smile. The only things that made Thiago smile like this were good food, coffee, and Benji, and no matter what his usually-stoic face may express, he was deeply happy to have this trifecta help him face the world each day.

The Skimmer's Keeper

Eight, nine, ten, eleven... Victor counted the rocks he'd stacked at the riverbed he frequented.

"Two more stones than last time!" he declared triumphantly. "Pretty impressive, wouldn't you say, Reedly?" he looked to his salamander-like pet. It peered back at him with a blank expression and a lick of its lips.

Reedly was a skimmer, a type of salamander with five pairs of external gills that moved like a mane of small tendrils. Skimmer colors ranged from blacks to pale greens that glowed fluorescently. Reedly was jet black other than the pearly white tips of her external gills.

"If you want Reedly to understand you and react, you're going to have to train her," Lewis didactically piped.

"How do you know if Reedly did or didn't understand me? And what would you know about training a skimmer?" Victor retorted, upset at Lewis's insinuation that Reedly was just a base animal.

Lewis shrugged nonchalantly. "I'm just saying — try teaching her a few commands." He bent down to pick at some of the petrified wood fragments along the river.

Victor begrudgingly made a sound of acknowledgement because as much as he was annoyed, he had to admit that Lewis knew quite a bit about marine animals. He'd met Lewis while exploring a brook near his home, becoming fast friends as two wanderers who preferred the outside over the walls of school. However, Victor was shocked that Lewis skipped school so often. *Do his parents not care? What about the school?* Victor himself was homeschooled by his moms. Ma Myrna was a proponent for student-centered learning pedagogies and Montessori methods, which she channeled into encouraging Victor to go out either alone or with them to experience the world. Mum Rory usually went along with whatever Ma wanted for his education.

It was also through Lewis that Victor learned trained skimmers were one of the government's most effective ways to maintain the ocean's pristine quality. Skimmers were used to contain any oil or hydrocarbon spills in the sea. A type of bacteria in the Marinobacter genus lived along their gills and within their intestinal lining, providing skimmers the special ability to degrade and process hydrocarbons. It made sense to Victor once he learned about this since he had found Reedly on a side of the road and discovered that she loved to spend time in his grandpa's auto shop. Ever since, Victor made a point to ask his grandpa everything about the substances he used to figure out what could be a treat for Reedly. He also dove into his local library to learn more about skimmers when he found that skimmers grew to be at least eight feet long. Since Reedly was just about two feet long, she was likely an infant-larvae.

"Anyway, I have to be off. I have to get home for lunch." Lewis bounded away, leaving Victor to his own thoughts.

He glanced at Reedly.

"Just you and me again, buddy." She stared back at him with unfocused eyes. Victor checked the time, then double checked that the item he'd been keeping in his pocket was still there before looking back at Reedly.

"What do you say to a trip to the aquarium?"

▼

The front of the Bellows Aquarium boasted a 55-foot tall sculpture of a red jellyfish that was illuminated at night, with its tentacles stringing down, an ode to the importance of the atolla jellyfish for society.

Reedly had wrapped herself around Victor's neck, like a travel pillow, with her feathery gills tickling his cheeks.

"Now, you behave, all right? Stay with me at all times," he chided at her before walking through the glass doors.

The metal arches within the doors chimed pleasantly, indicating it registered his person, and he was met with a *whoosh* of cool air. There were no admissions or ticket booths. Institutions such as the aquarium usually merely counted its visitors for traffic data. Upon entering, Victor found himself in the familiar domed structure with large nautical windows sprinkled along the perimeter, some as entryways into certain exhibits and some as large windows into various aquariums. The dome had a ring of a walkway along its circumference, splitting it into two levels. The second level offered smaller exhibits or a higher viewpoint of a large tank. The aquarium was designed to be like a starfish, with a central point and arms branching out, some straight and some bending and twisting.

Victor checked for the fifth time today that the item was still in his pocket and approached the information hub at the center of the dome.

"Is Jet in?"

The middle-aged lady looked up at him and glanced at Reedly before breaking into a bright smile.

"Aha! Vincent, right?"

"It's Victor," he corrected her politely, "but yes, it's me."

"Ah, silly me. I thought this time, maybe I got your name right since you had your skimmer with you, but I suppose I'll need to get my dosage of Reminserum sometime soon if I can't remember your name properly... despite you being a regular!" she chuckled to herself. She made an act of stabbing a syringe into her arm followed by a little jazz hands near her head to indicate the effect of the serum and laughed some more. Victor's parents never made a fuss about their Reminserum injections so the whole effect was quite comedic to him.

"Um, right." He pulled at his collar and laughed politely. "Is Jet here?" he repeated, stroking Reedly's tail that lazily hung down his shoulder over his chest.

The lady acted shocked. "Right! Sorry, I got carried away," she continued good-naturedly. "I'll check our maps. Sit tight."

As she consulted the light-up map built into the information desk console, with small bulbs indicating where tour groups were, Victor looked around the dome.

Less people today. That's nice. He disliked coming on field trip days. Parent chaperones inevitably tried to usher him into their groups, and he had to always do the same explaining of how he didn't go to their school. No, he didn't go to any other school here. No, he's not lost. He's homeschooled. No, he's not skipping school. Yes, his parents were quite aware of where he was.

"She's here," the lady interrupted his thoughts. "You're lucky! She's about to leave for a sabbatical, so today's some of her last tours."

Perhaps 'good timing' would be a better way to put it.

Mum Rory, a woman of few words, would say, "There's no such thing as dumb luck." Victor was sure she pulled this from somewhere else but understood what she left unsaid: Luck came to those who worked hard and were prepared to act on it. It's all about the timing and preparation. She didn't want him to think good things came about by nebulous, fickle luck.

And indeed, Victor had been coming every other day to try to catch Jet before she left; his hard work and consistency paid off today.

"Go to the Meridian Arm, and she'll be there," the lady continued. "I'll also give her a heads up that you're here." She gave Victor an unwanted wink which she probably thought was lightly mysterious as an adult and pointed toward the entrance that branched into the Meridian Arm section of the building.

One of the exhibits in the Meridian Arm were the giant isopods, one of Victor's favorites. The ghostly white armor of these foot-long pillbugs tickled his imagination. Of course, Victor knew they were crustaceans, but he liked to think of them as ginormous bugs, and he imagined riding the backs of the colossal six-foot long ones, a protected species, that lived deep within the ocean. Alas, the aquarium was only able to retain the smaller ones.

As Victor and Reedly stared at the isopods' unmoving forms, getting drawn in, he heard quick steps coming from behind and turned around. There stood Jet, looking ever the same with her long hair pulled into one low braid that she coiled around her neck like a scarf. Upon seeing him, she held her arms out wide and smiled.

He stuck a hand into his pocket for the item as he walked toward her.

"Hey Jet, I have something for you."

"Is that how you greet your merkin?" and the taller girl pulled Victor into a huge bear hug, ruffling his hair at the same time. Victor laughed while trying to escape her embrace, and Reedly transferred herself onto Jet while the two playfully wrestled. By the time Victor managed to pull away, Reedly had a head and two arms resting on Jet's head, the remainder of Reedly's body flowing down the back of Jet's head, over her left shoulder, and wrapping along her upper arm to secure itself. "Happy to see you too, Reedly," Jet said, reaching up to scratch Reedly's chin.

Merkin was short for 'Mermaid Kin'. This was a term given to those who were born from the same mermaid's purse, an external egg case used to develop embryos. These cases, or mermaids' purses, were reused from a specific oviparous shark species that created them to incubate their own young. Although extensively researched by doctors and scientists, this method of in vitro fertilization and incubation was not sponsored by the government. Moreover, the whole process was pricey, making mermaid children a rare occurrence, much less, finding a merkin. Despite negative stereotypes about mermaid children, children developed from mermaids' purses were no different from everyone else other than having a hidden iridescent birthmark. Placements and shapes of the birthmark varied depending on the specific mermaid's purse.

Victor had discovered the connection between himself and Jet at the aquarium very recently when he attended one of her guided tours. Jet had pulled her sleeves up to handle the isopods in the touch tanks, and Victor caught a glance of a shimmering mark on the inside of her upper arm near the elbow. Exactly where he had a birthmark that only shimmered when it was hit by light that went through water. When he had approached her, she was hesitant to show it to him until he showed her his own, and they found that they had the exact same mark. Victor's skimmer had also been interested in Jet from the get-go. Usually non-reactive, Reedly would flick her tail more fervently or try to climb Jet whenever she was around.

"I wasn't hugging you at first because I'm upset you're leaving." Victor huffed with a smile as he tried to fix his hair. Jet placed both hands on her hips and leaned back into a hearty laugh. Reedly leaned forward and placed a small sticky hand onto Jet's forehead to adjust to the change.

"Are you throwing a fit, Victor? Because that's *not* how to do a farewell!"

"No!" he vehemently denied and quickly looked away. "I just feel like we only just found each other. And now, you're leaving." Although their connection was discovered a mere three months ago, Victor already felt a familiar pull with Jet. She had immediately felt like an older sister he'd always had.

Jet stopped laughing and regarded him more closely.

"I know," she responded softly.

"But," Victor continued before she could say anything else. "I also know you have to do this. That this sabbatical is something you need."

Jet opened her mouth to say something, but nothing came out so Victor finally pulled the item out of his pocket.

"I don't know how long your trip will be, and I don't know what you're looking for. But I hope you find it. And..." he held his hand out to her. "I wanted to make sure you wouldn't forget your merkin," he smiled a bit at that, "so I made you something to help trigger recall."

He opened his hand, and in his palm was an isopod, carved out of wood. Along the spine, in a line of three, were small circles of inlaid mother-of-pearl. The contrast between the effervescent shimmer of the dots and the dark wood was startlingly gorgeous. Jet gasped and looked between Victor and the carved crustacean.

"You made this?"

Victor nodded. "It's just a small thing. Small enough for you to carry around."

Jet knelt with one knee in front of him, and instead of picking up the carving, she held his hand and the item together in both of hers.

"Victor, I wouldn't ever forget you. Even without seeing you often at the aquarium. And with or without Reminserum, I'll remember you. Through this." She pointed at her shimmering birthmark. "Because we both have it, it'll trigger my recall. I'll be back before you know it." When she released her other hand from Victor's, she left a small whistle made of nacre. It had been carved into the shape of a skimmer and strung into a necklace. "I wanted to give you this, too. I got this made for you by a windsmith friend."

It had a surprising likeness to Reedly. Although not jet black like her, the dark pearlescence with shifting greens translated well. Most impressively, the tips of the minuscule external gills became a white pearl, just like the white tips on Reedly.

"It looks just like her!" he exclaimed.

"Try it," Jet urged. Victor glanced around furtively.

"In here? Wouldn't we disrupt the other patrons?" he whispered. Jet shook her head.

"It's silent to our ears. No one will hear it. Except for..." she shifted her eyes up at Reedly who still had her head and arms on Jet's head. Victor inhaled sharply and felt an excitement bubbling inside his stomach. He picked up the whistle with his other hand, brought it to his mouth, and blew. Just as Jet said, Victor heard nothing except for his own breath pushed through the whistle, but Reedly was another matter.

Reedly stood straighter, supporting her own head rather than previously resting on Jet's, and her feathery gills stiffened and quivered as if listening intently. Her usually bulbous, vacant eyes were focused directly at Victor.

Victor ogled speechlessly at Reedly and then Jet. He'd never seen Reedly so attentive.

"What?" Jet demanded with brows raised. Victor looked at her again and pointed fervently at Reedly. Jet shot him an exasperated look and furrowed her brows. "Victor, what? What is it?" She shifted her eyes up to try to look. "I literally can't see because she's on my head. Just tell me!"

"It's Reedly!" he burst out. "She's listening!"

Jet chuckled as Reedly bristled playfully, adjusting herself on Jet's head so that her tail covered Jet's eyes.

"Oh good, at least we know the whistle works."

THE SEARCHING PHILANTHROPIST

"All right, well, I'm available anytime you need, okay?" Eli offered as the student stood up and collected her bags.

"Thanks, Mr. Elshzeng. I always feel better about," she waved in the air at some unknown entity, "all this after speaking with you."

Eli smiled. "How many times do I have to remind you to call me 'Eli'?" It always made him happy to hear he was having an impact and doing good work, especially for the future generation.

The student smiled politely and waved on her way out, after which Eli heaved a big sigh. Despite having chosen this path to get away from the high octane pace of his previous company, he thought this job was arguably more stressful — having to shoulder the worries and anxieties of teens experiencing the loss of their Kanperetinentia. His mind wandered to his own child. *Would I have counseled Luca the same way I'm counseling these kids on how to cope with this transition?* Before his mind spiraled him any deeper, he closed that door and gave an involuntary shudder. Twelve years of this, and he had gotten good at compartmentalizing.

Eli had left his job after a strange illness robbed him of his health and his young family twelve years ago. His heart and his life had disintegrated overnight; he felt and experienced nothing in his numb state for a few years before turning to fitness and using his child's education fund to purchase a small office building. From there, he got licensed as a counselor and kicked off his new non-profit. He previously made enough and proved his worth to the government so that he didn't need to worry about his living expenses for the rest of his life. But without a family with whom to share everything he had built, what was the point of saving? So, he threw everything he had into this new venture. Eli did what he did best: compartmentalizing his emotions, building a company framework, and finding smart ways to work, including applying for grants for his non-profit. He received some government funding as they recognized the work he was doing was valuable.

Although Eli was using skills from his corporate experience, if anyone from his previous life saw him on the streets these days, they wouldn't recognize him. Gone were the days of clean, short hairstyles and ironed suits. Eli sported shoulder-length hair that he pulled into a low ponytail, and his day-to-day wear consisted of wide t-shirts, baggy pants, and chunky sandals.

As his non-profit's clientele grew, he never charged anyone because to him, this service should be widely accessible. He wished they incorporated this into the school system. *But every thing has its lacking areas.*

He closed his file on the previous student and gathered his other folders to put away when he heard a knock at his door.

"You may cross," Eli responded without thought. When he looked up, he was thrilled to find Calvin, the hesitant 17-year old with whom Eli had been working. "Calvin!" he uttered in mild surprise. "It's not often you come on your own accord."

Calvin's foster parent had signed him up for Eli's services. She knew Calvin was highly intelligent and worried the loss of Kanperetinentia would deeply affect him. *Understandably so.*

From what Eli heard, his foster parent did the best she could, but wasn't allotted a higher education stipend for Calvin. However, Calvin always took that in stride and seemed to self-learn anything he needed. He performed well enough at school. Never failing a class, not ruffling any feathers, but also not excelling even when all his teachers seemed to see more in him.

"Hey, Eli," the teen scratched the back of his head apologetically. "I think, with, you know, the time nearing for me, I'm finally ready to start talking about it." Calvin noted Eli's gathered papers and quickly added, "I mean, I can come back another time if you're about to leave. I know it's the end of the day."

Eli immediately sat back down. "Not at all. I promised you I'm here to talk whenever you're ready, so here I am." *Thank, Mazu!* Inside his head, Eli was doing backflips, ecstatic that his months of trying to peek into Calvin's mind and praying to the sea goddess had finally paid off. He gestured at Calvin to sit at the plush chair across from him and offered a bowl of rasboiberries and sea grapes.

"Thanks, Eli." Calvin sank into the chair, and Eli waited patiently.

"My birthday is coming in two months," Calvin started. Eli remained silent. "And I can already feel it slipping," Calvin continued to his hands, as if he were visualizing sand slipping between his fingers.

"Your memories?" Eli made an educated and obvious guess.

"Everything I know," Calvin corrected. "I don't really care about memories. I can make new ones." Eli mentally noted this was a great and healthy mindset, while he himself grasped desperately to memories of his family.

"I'm losing knowledge," Calvin announced like some tragic hero. "Mostly short term items for now. Like things I read yesterday or discovered."

"Mmm," Eli nodded emphatically. "This is not abnormal, Calvin. If it makes you feel any better, it seems your loss of Kanperetinentia is progressing at a usual pace. It doesn't make it any less difficult, though. How do you feel about it?"

"I'm," Calvin paused before looking away. "I'm scared," he said in a small voice.

What a breakthrough! "We all go through this," Eli attempted to comfort. "The good thing is, once you turn eighteen, you'll have access to Reminserum, and that should help immensely. This transition period is probably one of the most difficult times you'll have to go through on top of finishing school. But remember there's also the mandated transition period so you have a year after this to adjust."

Calvin nodded absently. "Yeah, I know. But still. I'll actually have to make notes and keep files to refer back to. Like you." He added with a small grin.

Eli laughed heartily. "Oh, the horror!" and Calvin also bursted out laughing. "It's not too bad though, Calvin. It's an adjustment, but once you get in the habit of note-taking on top of taking Reminserum, it's not bad."

Calvin's face fell again, and Eli immediately regretted his words, wondering what he had said wrong.

"Hey, it'll be tough, but I hope you take solace in the fact that we all go through it, and we have resources for you. You've already done the hard part, which is acknowledging your emotions and seeking help here."

▼

By the time Eli bid goodbye to Calvin, closed his office, and got to his car, the sun was just setting, casting a purple-orange hue across the sky. Even though Eli had been pescatarian for five years, he had a craving today. Today, he really wanted to have the sesame oil chicken dish his late wife was so good at making. But he just couldn't get right.

Time to visit MAGMA. Eli leaned back in his car seat and breathed in before starting the car.

The Westway MAGMA location swarmed with people who were stopping by after their work hours. Eli swiped into the building with a wave of his palm over one of the standing kiosks scattered near the entrance and headed to an elevator to take him to the Memory Rooms. Memory Room Number Five was the first room Eli saw with its light illuminated, indicating it was free to use.

WELCOME, ELI ELSHZENG

The text showed on the seven-story high, dark, curved screens upon Eli's entrance. He positioned himself at the center of the circular room when he heard the familiar *whoosh* of the machinery below the floor settling into place to start.

SYNCHRONIZED

The text on the screen before him changed again.

You may extract whenever you're ready...

The ellipses on the screen blinked on and off, as if in anticipation. Eli closed his eyes and thought of his wife.

THE PERFECT DAUGHTER

Liz wrung her hands as she waited outside her father's office. She could hear his muffled voice inside, finishing his last meeting of the day. As she looked down, she wished she hadn't painted her nails a colorful array of iridescents. Her father had always found "unnatural" nail colors childish. Liz wanted to look older and responsible in her father's eyes, but she hadn't known he'd call her in today.

The massive double doors swung open, and an enforcer clad in her starched burgundy-purple uniform and bucket hat, gorgeously stitched and embroidered with gold thread, motioned for Liz to enter while a group of well-dressed adults exited. All of them ignored her except for Dr. Leo-Trisham who gave her a smile. Liz had always liked this woman. As for the others, Liz couldn't help but think they wouldn't ignore her older brother the way they did her.

"Father," she addressed Prime Minister Gio, "the next Coral Ball is not until the next full moon, so I wasn't expecting to see you today." The only times Liz saw her father as of late was when she accompanied him to official events.

Her father sat at his desk, poring over a book. Without a glance at her, he instructed, "Sit."

She sat at the couch in front of his desk and kept her posture as impeccable as she could, but she couldn't help but steal glances at the shelves behind his desk. They were filled with books and various curios, and it was always a treat to spot something new. This time, the newest curiosity was a shark skin leather-bound book with a built in latch and lock. A small, metal arm extended from the latch and ended in a set of round glasses with mother-of-pearl lenses. Liz thought of how they matched her nails.

Prime Minister Gio finally broke the silence.

"Tell me, Liz. Why are you drawing attention to yourself?"

"Excuse me?" Liz jolted her attention back to her father. Her father looked up at her.

"You are getting involved in multiple school clubs. Not just any school club, but acting and choir and singing." He had paused between listing each club activity for emphasis.

Liz suddenly felt a surge of emotion and clenched her fists.

"There's nothing wrong with those clubs. I'm keeping my grades up and maintaining my image for the family, like you always expect of us."

"Yes, but I don't need you traipsing around, performing and making the local news on your performance. You should be focused on your studies, not socializing."

"These clubs aren't *socializing*. It's an art. And I'm good at it. It's not my fault if I give a stellar performance through my hard work and practice, and a local news outlet wants to write a piece about it," Liz squeezed out through gritted teeth, trying to maintain her composure. If there was anything her father disliked, it was expressing strong emotions. "And wouldn't you say stage experience helps with being on the media as a part of this family?"

"To be a Bellows is to be humble and modest. We don't show off to the world. That's part of why our family is so beloved by the public."

For Prime Minister Gio and for the entire Bellows family, they were not only the political head of the nation, but they were also revered figureheads. People loved them, and so they were expected to be perfect — clear of faults, and that included always being calm, demure, professional, and gracious. But Liz never understood why her father wanted her to be quiet and blend into the background. *Isn't a part of being the perfect family to stand out and show the world all of my skills and accomplishments?*

"Look, Liz," Gio's expression softened, and he suddenly looked 20 years older before his perfect visage covered everything again. "I'm proud of you. I really am. I watched your performance."

Liz gawked at him. "You did?"

"Every time. I watch each one. I don't want to make a commotion of it at your school, so I go incognito," he grinned, "but manage it, please. You may partake in whatever activities you wish, but pick and choose when you're in the limelight and when you're not."

"Father," Liz pleaded, "I don't understand why! Anything else that you say or request, I get it and I do it. But I'm so confused by this. Why do I have to show up at all these high-profile events with you surrounded by media, but then I can't draw too much attention myself? I can't be like Bolmar!"

"Your older brother has nothing to do with this. And I'll... explain some other time." Gio looked tired again. "Just manage it, Liz. You don't always have to be the main protagonist. The supporting characters are good too — not the main focus, but still appreciated by the audience, right?"

"Is it because I'm a girl?" Liz seethed silently, shaking at Gio's non-answer.

Prime Minister Gio's eyes flashed while his jaws clenched, and Liz remembered why people in the administration feared him and immediately looked away. His arowana fish in the large tank built into the curved walls suddenly swam in a frenzy.

"Careful, Liz," he warned.

"I'm sorry, Father. I just... don't understand. And where's Bolmar? Why can I never see him?" Not only did she feel like she was always trying to live up to her brother's shadow, but it frustrated her even further that she barely ever saw him.

Gio got up and approached her, softly putting his hands on her shoulders and waited for her to meet his gaze.

"Bolmar is busy, and this is a separate conversation. I love you both equally very much. And no, it's not because you're a young lady. Bolmar is the eldest, and he should be taking on everything. I do not want the public's attention nor pressure on you."

She nodded mutedly. *When Father says it that way, I suppose he's trying to protect me...*

Liz hadn't seen her brother in years, and the fact he was busy was always the excuse. The only proof of his existence, both to the public and to Liz, was an occasional appearance at an event if Prime Minister Gio was occupied with other plans.

"Good," Gio thumped her shoulders. "Before you go, I have a challenge for you." His eyes twinkled as his private chefs came in bearing two steaming bowls of spicy, ramen noodles.

"Oh," Liz smacked her lips and grinned impishly. "You're on."

Liz treasured their spicy, ramen challenges, because only during these times did Prime Minister Gio become the father she remembered from a young age. As she's gotten older, she found him increasingly distancing himself from her, but these ramen challenges were moments when she had him back.

The Closer

SEOMRA

"What would you like today, Ms. Kammel?"

"Oh!" Seomra snapped out of her thoughts and focused on the coffee menu. The image of the seasonal aquamango latte drew her attention, and the barista noticed.

"The colors sold you, didn't it?"

Seomra laughed. "You know me." She dug into her baleen tote for her wallet.

"No, no. It's on the house," the barista held out a hand dismissing Seomra's wallet while ringing up the order with her other. "You're a regular. Don't worry about it. Plus, this gives me the chance to keep practicing getting the ombre orange-to-blue right!" She winked. "People get a bit scared of color sometimes, so I'm happy whenever someone orders it."

Seomra smiled graciously and mentally noted to herself to use this coffee shop for the next MAGMA meeting to put in a big order. Although she knew it wasn't the case, she didn't like owing people.

Her bracelet rang, indicating a work call, and she tapped her earring cuff piece to pick up while settling at a table. At the same moment, the coffee shop door chime jingled, and she glanced at the entryway.

Framed by the doorway, with the sunshine beaming from behind him, was a broad-shouldered man, smartly dressed in a brown suit with his sandy blonde hair done in a way that said, 'I'm professional, but also down to Earth and friendly.' He glowed with the sun's rays blessing his olive-toned skin. His gaze met Seomra's eyes and softened into a smile that brought out just the smallest wrinkles at the ends of his eyes. His dark brown eyes seemed to twinkle but were actually the subtle clouds of milky white swirling among his irises, giving away his occupation.

Ah, he must be one of the Memory Room engineers. But... they don't usually look like... this. At least, not at the branch I work at...

Since Seomra didn't break her gaze, he raised his eyebrows slightly, and instead of making his way to the front to order coffee, he started toward her.

Wait. What! He's coming over here! What do I do? Stay calm, Seomra. Look casual. Don't look phased. Shoot him a lovely smile or something. Oh gosh, I hope that smile didn't come out creepy. Okay, he's still making his way over so I guess it was okay. Oh my gosh what do I say when he gets here? How can he look even better as he gets closer? Am I blushing? Wait. What if he's not coming to me? What if there's someone behind me? No, get a hold of yourself, Seomra. You're hot. You're confident. It's you. A million thoughts whirled in her mind.

As he approached her, his hair and the flaps of his suit jacket blew back slowly, as if there were a slight wind blowing. *Inside the coffee shop?* Seomra's heart pounded faster as he drew nearer. As he slowly broke into a smile, his white teeth dazzled her and *sparkled?* Every small movement he made, the slight cock of the head, a quick glance downwards before meeting her gaze again, the brief jaw clench, were all magnified. The coffee shop faded into the background with the sunshine lighting only the approaching man. And the man? It was taking forever for him to get to Seomra even though they were only about ten strides away from each other.

I'm in a Memory Room! That's when Seomra remembered she was recalling a memory rather than living it in real-time. She refocused herself. She had been playing her memory of their first encounter in slow motion without realizing. She adjusted mentally so that the memory played at normal speed and smiled, both at the memory and at her own silliness. She'd come back to recall the memory to remind herself what that work call was about. Seeing as she had been distracted in the moment by the man at the coffee shop, she hadn't remembered what she talked about on the work call she picked up. But it seemed like she had gotten distracted again, even in memory.

"Oh, Seomra. You're so ridiculous," she chuckled at herself before ending the memory recall.

▽

"Seomra Kammel, the Closer," she answered the incoming call with practiced professionalism. Closers were product managers for the Memory Rooms at MAGMA. As the Closer for the Qamaria MAGMA location, Seomra was the liaison between GMA representatives and her engineers who worked in the Memory Rooms. Because of the numerous memories these engineers inevitably encountered while working, access between their work and others was limited to the Closer to handle. Whenever there was an issue with the technology, the Closer raised it. Whenever there was a directive from the government, the Closer communicated it to the engineers. Whenever there was an interesting memory recall as categorized by the handbook, the Closer noted it. Whenever the team had proposals for improving the product, whether it be latency or storage or user experience, the Closer presented it and advocated for it with the GMA.

Some say that the role's title 'Closer' came from the fact that they ensured the recalled memories stayed in the closed circuit of the Memory Rooms by managing the engineers and the memories. However, the name truly came from the fact that Closers closed memories.

By clipping them.

After her pilates class in the morning, Seomra dressed in her signature all-black. A sleeveless top with an elegantly stooped neckline paired with her flowy trousers and accessorized with a smart belt. She threw on some wedges and tied her long, straight black hair into a high, polished pony-tail.

She was early today, so Seomra took a scenic walk to her favorite coffee shop with the friendly barista to grab an aquamango latte for the road, and then took the corporate bus line to MAGMA.

By the time she got to MAGMA, people were already milling in, either to log into work or for a morning Memory Room session. The engineers were also already hard at work since the Qamaria location was open twenty-four seven. Seomra hovered a palm above one of the standing vertical kiosks scattered throughout the entrance and headed downstairs.

"Good morning, Kammel."

"Hey there, Kammel."

"Happy dawn."

"Morning, Seomra."

Various voices of the engineers greeted her as she entered, sparing her quick glances of acknowledgement before gluing their eyes back to their respective 24-inch curved screens.

"Anything to note from last night?" she asked them collectively as she set her bag down at her desk. These were the engineers from the night shift, and they should be switching out with the day shift engineers soon.

"Nothing to note," they answered in unison, continuing their work. Seomra nodded approvingly. She made sure to check the logs between shifts to confirm their reports, but with the years of experience among the engineers, she also trusted their gut. They had something she didn't have after all: the ability to read recalled memories in real-time.

Recalled memories in the Memory Room were retained for a short period of time, unless noted otherwise, to ensure citizen privacy. As such, Closers were important for reviewing the memories chosen by the algorithm for a second review. However, engineers could view the memories *while* people were recalling in the room, watching the memory with them from behind black screens. Engineers were able to do this because they have been genetically engineered for the Memory Rooms. As such, the engineers saw everything, whereas Closers only reviewed marked memories. Although genetically modified, Memory Room engineers looked and acted just like any other person outside the MAGMA Memory Rooms. The only differentiation from the general public were their brown eyes with swirls of gray moving within their irises. This change in eye color and the addition of the swirls was a side effect of the genetic alteration, as if the memories they viewed during work took a physical form and floated in their visions permanently.

Seomra turned on her work tablet and opened the file of memories marked for her review, noted by both the algorithm and manually by the engineers. *I hope I don't have to clip any from last night.* Seomra wished this to herself before each session of reviewing. In her seven years of work here, she'd only had to close three memory clippings, and it made her incredibly sad each time. A memory clipping was as its name suggested: a memory that had been cut from a person's memory bank to prevent recall of it forever.

"Think of it like a newspaper, filled with information, and we cut an article out. But instead of cutting it out for cherishing later, we lock this newspaper clipping away so that people won't read it when they go back to read the same newspaper," Seomra's mentor had explained in the past.

Yet, because of how precious memories were, Seomra didn't like closing memory clippings. She also understood, however, that maybe some memories weren't meant for keeping. Especially for the well-being of the government.

Seomra was 40 minutes into reviewing when the first engineers started logging out and gathering their belongings. Seomra looked up at the wall clock. *Shift is over already?*

"I'll see you all tomorrow," she called out. A few gave silent waves, and several called out a farewell before leaving. Although Seomra was on good terms with the majority of her engineers and had even hung out with multiple she'd call friends outside of work, she hadn't been able to shed the feeling of unnerve with their synced mannerisms at work or the way the silver-gray swirled in their eyes throughout these years, especially if they looked directly at her. That's why she was so shocked when the engineer at the coffee shop locked eyes with her. *It was different with him.* Although he had the same eyes, she had felt a comfort in his gaze.

Seomra jolted her attention back to the room as more people left. Each shift left and started at staggered times to ensure there was always someone to provide Memory Room services.

Seomra heard the first incoming steps. *First one of the day shift, I suppose.* She looked up and felt her breath catch in her throat.

"Nigel?"

His expression mirrored her surprise, but he gathered himself first.

"I guess they transferred me to your branch," and he broke into a large beam, wrinkling his eyes.

NIGEL

Nigel had missed his morning alarm, and that never happened. It shouldn't. It was built into his body to be on time for work. But he didn't have time to ponder that as he rushed through his morning routine. He figured he'd buy the office pastries for his tardiness since he was already late, so he ran to the nearest coffee shop.

That's when he saw her.

Nigel felt his whole morning slow down when he pushed open the doors and met her gaze, framed by long, dark lashes. She reflected his look of pleasant surprise before her mouth curved into a lovely smile. People usually didn't hold his gaze, especially not for this long. Without thinking, he made his way toward her.

She's looking at me, right? Yeah, she's not breaking eye contact, so I think it's okay to approach her. Right? Well, she's smiling bigger now. That's a good sign. Thank Mazu I put some effort into my looks today even though I was rushed. All right, Nigel, what are you going to say to her? 'Good day, ma'am. I couldn't help but notice you.' No, that's weird. She'll never talk to you again if you do that. Wait, I hope my breath doesn't smell. Gosh, well I'm here now.

"Hi," Nigel managed. *Dang it, say something else!*

"Hi," the woman responded, tucking a loose hair behind her ear while deftly tapping her earring cuff to end a call.

"Are you," he cleared his throat, "a regular here?" *You're going to start with* this, *Nigel?*

The woman's countenance brightened at that.

"I am!" She motioned to the image of a colorful latte on the wall menu. "They have the most interesting and nouveau flavor combinations. Plus, their coffee is good." Nigel felt himself relax at the warmth she exuded.

"Well, even though I live nearby, this is my first time here. Do you have any recommendations? I was going to grab a whole box of pastries for work." Nigel scratched the back of his head in embarrassment at being late. Her eyes rounded in interest.

"Work? If you don't mind me asking... your eyes..." she started as she focused her gaze onto his eyes as if trying to peer into his core.

"Oh," Nigel took a small step backwards, suddenly self conscious of his eyes that were a testament to his profession.

"Oh, sorry!" The woman put up both hands gently. "I was being a bit insensitive. I don't mean anything bad. I actually am a Closer, so I work with engineers. I was inquiring since I'd never seen you before at my branch." At that, Nigel loosened. She suddenly felt more familiar to him. He'd only ever met his own Closer, but they were some of the few people who treated his kind normally.

"Not at all," Nigel reassured her. "Usually, people outside work react strangely when they see my eyes close-up, so my reaction was an assumption on that. I apologize for placing that on you. My eyes used to be a hazel with a ring of brown before the modification, but I guess the brown color spread afterwards. That's neither here nor there though. Not really an important detail, I suppose. Just thought it may be interesting, but of course, you probably already know our eyes change with the operation." Nigel tried to make conversation but found himself blabbering before pausing and taking a breath to reset. "If you don't mind, may I join you for your morning coffee?" She smiled the prettiest smile, and Nigel felt his stomach do a flip.

"Only if you give me your name," she said playfully, motioning at the seat next to her.

He laughed, having forgotten all about work.

"Of course! Where are my manners? I'm Nigel Tillau. And you are?"

Nigel was glad he missed his alarm today.

The Questioning Deputy

The Incident

Hrisha was making her night rounds when she heard shuffling in the Artifact Room, a room with restricted access for just the Prime Minister, his family, and closest caregivers. She froze. *Who could possibly be here?* She relaxed into a familiar fight stance, keeping her center guarded, and raised her glowing whip that was coiled along her forearm. At times like these, she was grateful for the light the rope provided, but didn't like how it was also a shining beacon to her location, removing any element of stealth.

38 Hours Before the Incident

The cadet who just joined the Prime Minister's special forces entered the check-in room. Hrisha checked the time.

"Cadet Ricco, you have another 10 minutes to your lunch break," Hrisha addressed him. Cadets were not necessarily students. They were already seasoned enforcers, but because of the rigor and screening for the special forces, upon joining the team, they were demoted to cadet until they completed an additional year. As such, those in the special forces ranked higher than the usual enforcers and have a uniform with gold embroidery as opposed to silver. But that's the only difference in uniform. The string used for embroidery. Otherwise, all uniforms were a shade of burgundy-purple. Given that general enforcers go through thousands of hours of training, the special forces had received criticism for the tradition of demoting enforcers who join, but ultimately, it was still a coveted position.

"Deputy Sellue! I finished early," he stammered with his uniform's bucket hat in hand. "I figured I might as well come back and start my shift."

Having been a new special forces recruit years ago, she knew the feeling of trying to impress senior ranking enforcers within the first week.

"Skipping parts of your lunch will not result in an expedited promotion, Ricco. I'd hope you're not thinking I'd give you special favor?" Hrisha raised a brow.

He dropped his hat and squeaked, "That's not what I meant! I mean, yes I want to work and move up the ranks of the special forces. But that's not why I came back early, ma'am. I just want to do a good job!" he spluttered quickly.

Hrisha dropped her stern expression and started shaking with silent laughter. She found it amusing to scare the cadets early on.

"You're fine, Ricco. At ease," she managed between her laughs that finished into a chuckle. Ricco visibly relaxed. "But I'm serious. There's no reward for coming back early, so just take your whole break. Set this habit, and you'll thank me later when you're a fully fledged special enforcer with many tasks at hand. Although this job is important, it's good to set boundaries and stick to a schedule."

"Yes, ma'am!" he smiled gratefully and hastened away.

"Not that this job is incredibly stressful," Hrisha thought to herself as he left. She'd toiled to get into the enforcer program, transferred into the special forces, and risen in the ranks. Throughout this time, unrest, fights, or wars have never been issues as far as she could remember. The enforcers were around for community service and to help civilly solve disputes. The special forces specifically served the Bellows family and was a wanted position due to the closeness to the Prime Minister. No one outside the role really knew what they did, but now that she was in, she found that they guarded the family (*from what though?*) and guarded specific rooms of valuables. Occasionally, an enforcer will be sent on a secret mission, but it was usually errands (ranging from mundane to important) for Prime Minister Gio or his family. Typically, the special enforcer was sworn to secrecy and made to forget the mission. Loss of recall was so normal that no one thought more of it.

"You know you don't have to scare the cadets, right?" a voice broke her from her thoughts. She refocused and saw a friendly face, dressed in the white dimensional engineering division uniform.

"Carlisle! What are you doing in the enforcers' area?"

"What can I say?" he grinned. "Dimensional Engineers are granted higher clearance than enforcers." Hrisha guffawed and crossed her arms genially.

"You know that's not true with special forces enforcers." She threw up her hands. "If you don't want to tell me, that's fine. I know your wife is a big shot around here so you probably get extra perks to enter all sorts of rooms."

"Accusing me of nepotism?" Dr. Carlisle Trisham put a hand to his heart in the pretense of hurt. Hrisha laughed loudly. As Carlisle watched her laugh, he dropped his hand, and his look darkened briefly. "Even though our whole government is an empire of nepotism," he continued in almost a whisper, shrouded by her laughs. She stopped abruptly.

"Sorry? What was that?" *Did I hear that wrong?*

He looked back at her with a wide smile. "Nothing at all! I admit my wife is a genius in her field, but give me some credit, too, will you? Tell me, how's your family?"

Hrisha noted his attempt to change topics but let it go. She's known Carlisle and his wife for years, and if she wanted, she could ask him about this later. If she remembered.

After Carlisle and Hrisha chatted briefly, ending with an invite to the Trisham house for dinner on the weekend, Hrisha continued her tasks.

Considering how much work it took to get to her position and the value placed on it, it was a surprisingly low-stakes job. The Bellows family had around-the-clock monitoring, but there were enough enforcers to rotate shifts so it wasn't all bad. Hrisha got a night shift about once every two months. There were night shifts at MAGMA as well just to make sure everything was running smoothly. Occasionally, there would be some high school pranksters trying to pull a last stunt before the big 18, before losing their Kanperetinentia, but that wasn't a big deal.

Hrisha wasn't complaining, though. It was nice to take it slower, and she was happy to get some facetime with the Prime Minister. It was mostly the captain who communicated with him, but as deputy, Hrisha got to attend the majority of the meetings as the captain's right hand man — or woman. When the captain was unavailable or tending to other matters, then the Prime Minister called upon Hrisha. She often reminded herself that it was a prestigious position. She knew her parents were proud of her. Because of her job, her parents also received a higher stipend for better quality foods and lifestyle. Although they had decent jobs and hadn't struggled to put food on the table thanks to Universal Food Care, Hrisha could not deny that once she started working for the Prime Minister, the food they received changed into whole wheats, produce of greater variety, organic produce, and more fresh food rather than processed or pantry items. Food deliveries were also more frequent to ensure the freshness of the groceries. Her dad had been ecstatic when this started as he was an avid home cook. Thinking of her parents living happily and well taken care of after decades of their hard work made Hrisha's heart swell with emotion.

She'd made it.

One Hour Before the Incident

Thirty more minutes before I can log out of the building. Hrisha had switched shifts with another special enforcer today because that enforcer had some family matters that had come up. As deputy, a lot of her work was now administrative, but she still appreciated walking the halls and keeping up her skills. Moreover, it would be embarrassing if a cadet could beat her in one-on-one combat so when she finished her responsibilities, she always went to the enforcer gym to practice form, to do some cardio, and to train.

Before logging off, she planned to stop by the lounge to check the enforcer report logs throughout the sectors to see if there was anything worth reporting back to the Prime Minister (learning what to vet for him was important), and then hit the enforcer gym to train with the wingchun beams.

The special forces lounge was almost as luxurious as the Prime Minister's office. As Hrisha entered, the warm lights nested in sconces along the walls gradually lit the room. The lounge had pods for naps or meditation, clusters of couches for socializing, a kitchenette in the corner, and computer hubs. The computer hubs were two-by-two cubicles, making each hub a cluster of four computers, scattered across the room like little study groups. Every computer station was lit by small, antique green lamps. To the other side of the lounge was an expansive, waist-height tank of potamotrygon leopoldi stingrays, which doubled as a communal table where they had team meetings. Hrisha remembered being disconcerted by the black-and-white dotted disks lazily swimming beneath the clear tabletop holding her papers when she first started this job, but now she found them quite soothing to watch.

Suddenly, a tingling sensation started at the base of Hrisha's scalp, warning her that she wasn't alone. She whipped around toward where she felt a gaze on her.

"Deputy Sellue. I wasn't expecting you." It was Deputy Nikigaya, a special enforcer who had joined two years before Hrisha. The initial alarm subsided within Hrisha's chest at the recognition.

"I usually come in before my shift ends to check on logs. I switched shifts with another today to help out." Hrisha paused as something tugged at the back of her mind. "I... wasn't expecting you here either, Deputy Nikigaya. If I recall correctly, isn't your shift tomorrow?" *I'd just had my Reminserum dosage so I shouldn't be recalling inaccurately.* She kept her face passive as she made her way toward Deputy Nikigaya and his computer hub.

Strange... shifts are relatively strict. Why is he here?

As Nikigaya straightened to his full height, Hrisha didn't miss the swift and subtle movement of his right hand as he seemed to navigate his screen to something else before she approached.

"You are recalling inaccurately," Nikigaya said matter-of-factly. Hrisha expected this response and knew it was not true. She also knew Nikigaya wasn't the type to speak bluntly to for answers. Deputy Nikigaya had a reputation for intentionally elusive communication that always seemed to place other special enforcers in trouble, yet the senior leadership turned a blind eye. Carlisle's quiet remark on nepotism earlier briefly surfaced in her mind before she dismissed it. Hrisha had made it a point to avoid working with Deputy Nikigaya and hoped their two year difference in tenure excused her from being a threat in Nikigaya's eyes to stay off his radar.

A cold shiver ran down her spine as she observed Nikigaya measuring her in steely, calm regard.

"Well, I suppose misremembering happens." Hrisha feigned ignorance. "Does that mean you're the enforcer relieving me of duty early?" she added, testing him.

Nikigaya's right brow raised ever-so-slightly.

"I am not, Deputy Sellue. If you've switched for the night shift, you still have another thirty minutes. Although I'm not here for a shift, I am here for another purpose above your paygrade."

Hrisha internally scoffed at his attempt to subdue her with rank and drew to her full five-foot-eleven-inch frame, closely matching Nikigaya in height.

"Need I remind you, Deputy, that we are of the same rank?" Her eyes glinted dangerously while her expression remained smooth. She wasn't sure why he was being difficult, but her senses told her he was hiding something. *Nikigaya is skilled with the* sodegarami, *a nasty weapon, but I know I can take him weapons-free.* She continued to close the distance between them slowly.

Suddenly, Nikigaya put up both hands.

"You don't need to get all hostile on me, Sellue." His lips curled into a soft smile. "I'm merely carrying out a mission from the Bellows family. One of those missions of which details I cannot divulge, no matter to whom. You know the nature of our work." His tone took an apologetic tinge. This caught Hrisha off guard, and Nikigaya took the opportunity her pause gave him. "I will be taking my leave then." Lifting two fingers to his gold-embroidered burgundy bucket hat, he gave a half-salute and stepped out of the lounge.

His computer screen was still lit from earlier usage, so Hrisha stepped around to take a look.

It displayed the typical Government Memory Association home screen. She tapped the side of the device to have its camera tracker lock onto her eyes to navigate the screen and see if he left any documents open, but nothing came up. It was not in Hrisha's nature to snoop, but she wanted to settle the uneasiness she was feeling. Looking at the screen, she opened its logs to pull what Nikigaya was accessing, but she found very normal records and files.

Am I missing something? She shook her head. *I'm probably overthinking it. Nothing ever happens anyway. Nikigaya is just... a strange character in our forces.* She straightened her back and went back to her hub to check sector logs as she had planned before closing out her shift.

The Incident

No one should be in the Artifact Room. Hrisha had raised her glowing rope in preparation. Her shift was just about to end, so she was heading out when she had detected unnatural noises. She excelled at close combat, but the rope was useful for longer range attacks. She slinked along the walls like a shadow, making her way to the closed door. Because access was highly restricted, she didn't have the clearance for the room, but no one from the Prime Minister's family should be here at these hours.

With the hairs standing on the back of her neck, Hrisha knew she wasn't wrong and did not hesitate. Like a spring, she shot her elbow wrapped in her glowing ropes into the keypad panel and shattered it.

I'm making a lot of noise, but this room only has one entrance, and that's this one. They have nowhere to go.

Collecting her energy into her core, she rammed her shoulder into the door at a specific angle. At the same time, tiny eyes opened at the end of her glowing rope which slipped into the small gap Hrisha had made on impact. In one smooth motion, the snakelike rope unlocked the door mechanism while Hrisha slammed into the door, swinging the door wide open.

She sprang into the dark room, her tall outline dominating the doorway, and her face illuminated by her animated rope which had unraveled itself into three thinner ropes that stood attentively on end, like three eels standing sentry before her.

"There's nowhere to hide or run. Show yourself and perhaps we'll lighten the offense for this bit of honesty," Hrisha declared firmly.

She let the silence hang in the air for a moment before taking a step forward. She had always been curious about this room, but she was currently focused on apprehending the trespasser. As she stalked forward, like a predator testing its prey, she kept an eye on the doorway as well. She knew that as she stepped farther into the room, it was possible that the trespasser might make a run for the door. And that was exactly what she was counting on.

A dark, lean figure shot out of the darkness to her right toward the light of the open doorway, but Hrisha was faster. On instinct, she pivoted and using her torso's momentum, shot her ropes with her right arm toward the figure.

The figure yelped and grunted as the ropes wrapped around his legs and he hit the ground. As he struggled, the ropes continued lengthening, pulling his arms to his body to fully immobilize him.

"I bet you thought you were clever, huh?" Hrisha approached the masked, still figure on the ground. "Take off the mask," she instructed her ropes.

They obediently snaked up the figure's neck and pulled off the mask that was covering the lower half of his face. In their glowing light, Hrisha made out a familiar figure usually clad in white uniform and felt her fingertips grow cold as confusion gripped her heart.

"Carlisle?" she breathed.

THE SNACK SHOP OWNER

Saya Toniolee had inherited the small snack shop from her grandmother. Saya and her partner had lived in the city, but upon visiting the shop in the rural town, both of them fell in love. Saya was drawn to the slower pace of life, the fresh air, and the warm community of the town. When they visited, multiple neighboring shop owners had come by with bags of vegetables as welcoming gifts, giving kind words and sharing memories about her grandmother.

Her partner, Leopold, fell in love with the knick-knacks in the shop as he enjoyed tinkering. Plus, it hadn't hurt that he was immensely popular with the older neighboring ladies who had stopped by bearing gifts. They immediately acted familiar with him, asking for his help in various more laborious tasks. Saya had laughed at the time when he shot her a helpless glance while being surrounded by stooped, boisterous ladies. *That's what happens when you're the life of the party!*

After discussion upon returning to the city from their bucolic visit, they both felt that moving was the right call. Leopold had a remote job so he could work from anywhere, and Saya ran a small online tutoring business. The countryside felt like a great place to raise a child if it worked out, as well.

Most of all, Saya didn't want to let go of her grandmother's snack shop. Her childhood was filled with memories of running through the shop, hearing her small feet thumping on the wooden floors while her grandmother stocked the candies, snacks, and tiny toys, yelling out at the neighborhood kids to grab a few extras for the road. Smelling the hinoki wood, seeing the yellowing paper on the door screens, and hearing the wrinkling of the snack packages when she revisited brought Saya back. She wanted to keep the place alive.

Leopold had joked that they were escaping their corporate city life while they drove out to the town with their packed belongings, but Saya thought there may be a truth to that. She was tired of the city bustle, of the polished image everyone presented on the streets, of the advertising signs that yelled in their large font sizes and their garish colors throughout the city, of her friends' conversations surrounding their next business venture or in a bragging competition about their most recent vacation. Her soul was exhausted.

When she told her circle of friends that she and Leopold had decided to move to the countryside, they all stared at her, aghast.

"Why would you want to do that when we have everything here?" a friend had asked.

It's precisely that. Why is it that if we have everything here, I still feel like we're missing something. Something important. She'd given them a fluff answer along the lines of embarking on a new adventure.

That wasn't a lie, though. She loved her fantasy books, and moving to save her grandmother's snack shop felt like a piece of it. Like her chance to live a fantasy as well.

"I'm glad we don't have to worry about housing," Leopold's comment snapped Saya out of her reverie. "Like how fun will it be to live on top of the shop?" he continued excitedly. She loved him for this energy.

She cracked open a car window and breathed in the crisp air as they exited the city. This was the first time she'd felt alive in a long while.

Once again, the neighboring shop keepers had stopped by when Saya and Leopold arrived, offering their help or food. The neighbor in the nextdoor shop that specialized in meat buns had heard that Saya was vegan, and after profusely asking questions on what exactly Saya could have, had shuffled away quickly. He returned within the hour, presenting her a wax paper bag of another three steaming buns.

"Sorry, Mr. Moraima," Saya took the bag gratefully. "I won't be able to have these, but Leopold, my husband, enjoyed the ones you brought earlier!" The older man shook his head quickly and took on a shy smile.

"No, no. I just made these. They should be what you call," he paused as he recalled the word, "vegan. No meats or eggs. I used mushrooms, tofu, edamame, and some soaked vermicelli noodles and adjusted the flavoring so it works." He gulped nervously. "If you don't mind trying it?"

Saya couldn't quite place it, but she felt a lump in her throat as she considered the kind, elderly man who had been making steamed meat buns for six decades, who had ran back to his shop to make something completely new just so that she could have some. A warmth ran up from deep within her core to the back of her eyes, and she felt the tears building. She stayed silent for a few seconds, holding back the tears while the man looked up at her patiently.

"Yes," Saya sniffed once. "Absolutely, I'd love to try it. Thank you for making something for me." She picked one up and dropped it immediately at the heat that scalded her fingertips. Mr. Moraima laughed.

"Ah, yes, they are still piping hot. But that's also when they taste the best. Use a napkin or use the paper bag to hold onto it," he advised.

At this, Saya carefully maneuvered one of the buns from outside the bag, shuffling it up so that a third of it was exposed at the opening for a bite. She blew on it a few times as the older man's eyes grew wide in anticipation.

The bite of the bun was still hot in her mouth, so she kept her mouth open, sucking in a few breaths to help cool it. *But my goodness. This is SO good.* The steamed portion of the bun was fluffy and didn't stick to the teeth, and the filling! It was surprisingly juicy and flavorful, with a bit of a bite to the texture. Saya hadn't thought that minced mushrooms and tofu could taste like this with this kind of mouthfeel.

"Mr. Moraima," Saya said between bites, holding a hand up to her mouth to cover it out of courtesy, "it's amazing."

The elderly man's leathery face broke into a toothy grin.

"I'm glad I still got it!" he chuckled. "Well, you enjoy. If I make it a regular on my menu, maybe I'll call it the 'Sayabun'," and he excused himself, hobbling quickly back to his shop.

Saya watched him go, clutching the wax paper bag to her chest, and once he had left, she let the floodgates behind her eyes open and let the tears flow.

▽

"Oh, to live Grandma's simple life." Saya stroked an aged family photo. It depicted them in front of the snack shop, her grandmother standing behind a tiny Saya, with her arms wrapped lovingly around Saya and eyes wrinkled into the most joyous smile. Saya's mother and father flanked both of Grandma's sides with arms wrapped around Grandma's back. Her father smiled down at Saya, while her mother looked at Grandma affectionately.

Saya placed the framed photo back onto the shelf. She'd tidied the shop front for a few days before now tackling the storage room. In the few days since they'd moved in, Saya found that Grandma had placed at least one photo of the family in each room. Upon realizing this, Saya wished she'd visited Grandma more often in her adult life.

She pulled a box off the shelf and found it filled with small, plastic toys. *Extra inventory for the shop, I suppose. I'll bet Leopold will love rummaging through these.* Saya left the box on the floor for her partner and reached up to pull down the next box. As she pulled it off the shelf, her eyes caught a flash of movement. A piece of paper that was under the box had slipped out from underneath and dropped to the ground unnaturally with a metallic *clink.* Saya bent to set the box down and pick up the paper.

Huh, an envelope? She opened it and pulled out a photograph. Although in pristine condition, the colors had faded. It was a group photo of 20-or-so adults, all in trench coats like a kind of uniform, and they all had on silly expressions and poses. Saya thought they looked like a fun group.

Hold on... one of the people in the photo caught Saya's attention, and she brought her face closer to better scrutinize the faded photo.

Could it be?

With the envelope and photo pinched between her ring finger and middle finger, Saya reached for a photo album she had found earlier and flipped through furiously until she found the younger pictures of Grandma. She brought herself to a kneeling position on the floor and placed the open album on the floor, holding the group photo up to it to compare.

The face that caught her attention in the group photo was undoubtedly her grandmother, albeit younger than she remembered. Saya's breath hitched in excitement. She'd thought her grandmother lived in this town her whole life and ran the shop after her great-grandparents, but these people wearing those trench coats were definitely not something you see around this town. *Who would have known Grandma went somewhere else for school? Or an academy? Or something! Did she move away and come back? Like me?*

Once again, Saya wished she had visited her grandmother more often. She sighed in resignation at the answers she'll never get to know as she remembered the *clink* of metal when the envelope had fallen and the weight she felt between her fingers. She turned her attention back to the envelope and emptied it. Out fell a key.

Saya unclipped the ring of keys from her jeans belt loop and held both up. The unknown key had the same small logo engraved on it as the key she had that opened the vending machine right outside the shop. She put the two side-by-side to check if the teeth lined up. *They do! Is this a duplicate key?*

"If it's simply a duplicate, why was it in an envelope on its own?" a small voice questioned inside her.

Saya looked more closely at both keys again, and noticed this time that the unknown key had a few more grooves within the blade. *Curious.* She glanced at the group photo with her grandmother on the open album and back at the unknown key.

Maybe Grandma's life wasn't as simple as I'd thought...

Saya stood with the unknown key in hand, and headed outside toward the vending machine.

Acknowledgements

I want to thank the seven people who were pivotal to making this happen: Christina Chiu, Hailin Wang, Jeet Singh, Kyoko Tsuzuki, Letty Trevino, Ryan Chen, and Tommy Tang. These individuals believed so deeply in my first book that they committed to creating a character with me as a fun exercise to expand the world I created. Yes! I created these characters with them! Initially, I had planned to just share each character's story with their respective person, but as I wrote and developed these characters, I thought, why not share it with the rest of you? And then I added one of my own as I got a bit carried away.

I hopped on calls with these seven gems to create their characters' cores, and from there, the majority gave me free reign. For that, I thank you. Thank you for believing in me and doing this activity with me (and for your patience and trust!). If you're curious, you can refer to the Appendix for the notes I took during our calls to see how it all started and developed.

Thank you to my sister, Bug, for editing this novella-anthology, and for being my biggest hype man. Thank you to Bojana Gigovska, my cover artist, for going through numerous iterations with me and taking all of my feedback and inspiration images to create this beautiful design. She's outdone herself again! To my Bookstagram community — all of you Bookstagrammers and indie authors are inspirations to me — thank you for the fun and space you've all created. And thank you to my incredible team of beta readers: Sam Blatchford, Haewon Park, Sunny Sridhar, Kyoko Tsuzuki, and Andy Yu.

The critical feedback and affirmations they provided pushed me to finish this series.

Lastly, thank you to the readers and supporters who picked up this book and glanced into the lives of these characters. Thank you for all of your support and excitement for this companion novella installment with *The Vending Portal*. Not all characters get to have their moments to shine in a book, so I loved that this project allowed me to highlight a few and throw in some easter eggs. I hope you found as much joy and intrigue in these characters as I did!

Appendix of Scanned Notes

See if you're able to match the notes to the characters' final stories! Though sometimes the name suggestions are a dead giveaway...

Notes 1.1

- middle-aged (early 40s) / successful executive
- corporate worker — climbing
- jaded / disillusioned.
- moved away from corporate

NOW: - working w/ ppl in poverty
    - nonprofit.

- man
- fruits / vegetables / health nut.   → fruits / berries is favorite
    types
- pescatarian
- longer hair
- raggedy clothes → hipster
- had a family but due to illness → lost faith → long time ago
- kid (wife   ) (daughter) young.

☆ - found peace w/ current job. / found sense of purpose.
    trying so hard before to distract himself.
        from tragedy

clue / person - someone he's helped before (school age boy middle school)
    - helped w/ mentoring

- chill person, confident, straightforward, understanding
- farming (does farming)
- in down time — will play guitar in public. → bluegrass folk also sings
- photos of family w/ him
- has a necklace w/ cross on it.
    - Christian - vegetarian
    - Christian community   } not necessarily base religions in the world's religions

- slice of life
- Eli (last name) (made up)
- cool sandals.   Sam's sandals.

Notes 1.2

Age :
Sex : male.

man
- finding food
- a gourmet.
- 20-30 yr old.
- not in a bar
- mystery sexuality
- never actually
  say it's his kid.
- look for new
  experiences &
  culture.
- anything for food
- tree w/ peach in middle
  of nowhere - do that!
- jazz is favorite music
- purple is fave color.
- no favorite food

child.
- nephew
  childsize - Benji
- adorable.
- stuffed bear
- thoughtful. / nice
- charismatic.
- refer to ousama
  Ranking main
  character.

- simple aesthetic.
- old school asian
- sandals farmer
- undershirt wt
  raggedy
- "breathable."
- clean cut.
- pompadour hair
- clip on tie
- looks poor so
  no one let him in
  vast food knowledge.
- food critic
- travelling kid for delicious food
  - freelance food critic.
- talk to kid like adult.
  - funny care for kid.
  - bounce ideas off kid.

- ground break.
  light roast.
- must drink
  coffee.
- slow enjoyment
- comments on
  notes of coffee.

- offers it to the
- kid   kid.

- allergic to
  the food he's
  been searching for

Notes 1.3

- female — mid to late 20s/early 30s
- quieter, interested in learning
  - understanding the "why?"
- presents friendly but questions a lot
- has partner/lots of friends / 2 pets
- enjoys outdoors → picnics/hike/explore
  - does fun things w/ partner & pets
- likes gardening/growing things
- cooks
- fantasy books, she likes
  - escapism ——→ all her hobbies are about escaping (not just for fun)
- mainstream music classical→likes
- darker complexion, lighter eyes
- petite woman
- casual wear: jeans, athleisure, comfy sweaters

→ Partner: darker complexion, male.
  handyman, tinkers in garage, makes things
  social butterfly / life of the party.

- makes a life-changing discovery about her family that makes her question everything's she's done so far.

related: escaping from this discovery.

Notes 1.4

- 17 yrs old.   *asexual / not in marriage.
- female. / above avg height but not exceedingly tall   5'8"
- prime minister's daughter.
- position run in family for long time
- apprenticing w/ Gio
- but she's questioning it. but about to lose memory.
- fear of growing up / responsibility
- perfectionist.
- black sheep.
- short pixie hair   ☆ - paint fingernails
                                   colorful fingernails
- likes femme like eyeliner but likes
      plaid, grunge outfits
- natural leader but anxious.
- have a friend or diary to have conversations
  (adopted daughter.) - older bro who's
      never seen.
        - frustrated she's not the heir
- she always accompanies her father
      to events.
- ~~????~~
- singing. / choir. / acting.
- spicy food / her + her Dad like to compete
- a bit rebellious. - goes out to talk politics
- punk

Notes 1.5

Calvin ~~Dregs~~ : male   17 years old.
Hobbies :

Does whatever he can to earn $
Foster

- Hispanic
- First layer. // second layer.
- Loves horticulture. & plants. → dealt in drugs & developed ♡ for plants   @ age of
- grandma old envoy.   Lo content for memory   17. so losing
- skater.   memory.
- loves foster parents : since 14.   - ~~Happens road~~
- drug $ to fund greenhouse. @ envoy compound   - stroke of ~~genius~~
- flashback?   - now going over
- underdog genius   voices but losing
- quiet, thoughtful, introverted, gets jobs done.   it.
- nose : vending machine cinnabuns is favorite food.
- 5'8"   hair matted head : like coco kid
- ripped jeans, sneakers, jacket, carries old backpack.
        - canvas sneakers
- dislike center of ~~attn~~.
- street smart
- stole library books – self taught organic chemistry.
        - 3 books : Horticulture
                 early pharmacy
               " orgo. Organic chemistry.

Notes 1.6

- 25 yrs old   wants a partner
- female, hetero. ← talking to a few ppl.
- single.
- consultant / the closer. / to get stuff run.
- city-contemporary - black favorite color.
- not a big music fan
- business → athleisure aesthetic.
- race can decide.
- pilates everyday.
- order diff coffee every time
       -gravitate to drinks that look unique
           like ombre to try
- weekday
- alone / no pets / no plants.
- try different things
- scorpio.

---

rtes: online game.

- tall, introverted comes off as confidence/suave.
- "not interesting enough"
- steady, calm, funny.
- well-read
- works on Halo - video game testing
- loves rules
- looks friendly.
- thinker.
- super hot.
- green eyes / closer to pupil → Hazel-brown.
- dirty blond/sandy

Notes 1.7

About the Author

Inspired by her love of Marvel, sci-fi, old Taiwanese dramas, and ridiculous anime, Judy scribbles mini-stories wherever she can (and subsequently forgets them!). She graduated from Rice University in Houston, Texas, studying history, Asian studies, and education. Judy is not unfamiliar with extensive writing, having published multiple pieces. She spent some time living in rural Japan before working in the legal and compliance sp here.

With her debut novel *The Vending Portal*, Liu hopes to meaningfully add to Asian American literature to further enrich the YA genre.

Outside of work and writing, Judy enjoys dancing with her teammates and friends, exploring unknown spots or cities, frequenting coffee shops with her tiny pup, and making nonsense sounds to her sister.

To learn more, you can find her on Instagram (@judyliu_author) or visit her website www.judyliua uthor.com.

www.ingramcontent.com/pod-product-compliance
Lightning Source LLC
Chambersburg PA
CBHW060506300726

48975CB00008B/2676